HARD CORE
LOGO

HARD CORE LOGO

MICHAEL TURNER

ARSENAL PULP PRESS
VANCOUVER

Dedicated to the memory of the California Golden Seals.

HARD CORE LOGO
Copyright © 1993 by Michael Turner

SECOND EDITION Copyright © 1996 by Michael Turner

ARSENAL PULP PRESS
103-1014 Homer Street
Vancouver, B.C.
Canada V6B 2W9

The Publisher gratefully acknowledges the assistance of the Canada Council and the Cultural Services Branch, B.C. Ministry of Small Business, Tourism and Culture.

All songs copyright © by Michael Turner, Hard Core Logo Music, Colonel Festus Publishing, SOCAN, 1993

Some of the narratives in this collection were first broadcast on CBC Radio.

Photos and cover photo by Ingrid Percy
Author photo by Judy Radul
Typeset by the Vancouver Desktop Publishing Centre
Printed and bound in Canada by Kromar Printing

CANADIAN CATALOGUING IN PUBLICATION DATA:
Turner, Michael, 1962-
  Hard core logo

    ISBN 1-55152-033-8

    I. Title.
PS8589.U748H37 1996   C813'.54   C96-910485-5
PR9199.3.T838H37 1996

CONTENTS

ACKNOWLEDGEMENTS

MY TOP 100-PLUS LIST includes: Ingrid Percy (for her love), my family (for theirs), Brian Lam (for his editorial input), Wendy Atkinson (for her promotional efforts) and Patty Osborne (for her professionalism).

The musicians: the Animal Slaves, the Battered Wives, Art Bergmann (mortgage-payment bar bill), Billy Bragg (ditch the band), Meryn Cadell (return my calls), Johnny Cash, the Clash, Phil Comparelli (helped me eat a handful of dirt once), Stompin' Tom Connors (outdrinks everyone), Country Dick (drank our rider), Country Joe, cub, Devo, the Dils (and what came next), DOA (that was now, this is then), Elvises, David Gogo (Fender Mustang, heavy gauge), Gun Club, the Guthries, Gerry Hannah (eats at the Frontier), Hard Rock Miners, Joe Hill, Chris Hillman, Jr. Gone Wild (featuring 'Mom' Simmons), Hudie Ledbetter (will tune your 12-string while you sleep), Lost Dakotas, Luther Victim (try their "Cavernous Roll"), Ewan MacColl, Malcolm's Interview, Meat Puppets, the Modernettes, the New York Dolls (why Buster, David?), the Nips (get back, Shane!), Herald Nix, Phil Ochs, Gram Parsons, the Picketts, Pointed Sticks, the Ramones (fuck the guitar solos), Jimmy Rankin (thanks for the cigarette), Jean Redpath, Rheostatics (too good for their own good), Keith Richards (share your millions), Jeannie C. Riley (country music P.T.A.), Roots Round Up (for getting Ford on waivers), Kevin 'Lemon Loaf' Rose, the Saving Grace, the Seegers, Show Business Giants ('cause I was paid to say it), Slow (the Hamm years), the Smugglers (the Roman Candles of Canadian pop), the Smiths, SNFU, the Sons of Rhythm Orchestra (and Jerry Jerry), Subhumans (always already), Teenage Head, the Undertones (right, Ike?), the Velvet Underground, Violent Femmes, Rufus Wainwright, John Williams (not *that* John Williams), Lucinda Williams, Robert Wiseman, X (the Knitters, too) and Neil Young (please make more inaccessible music).

The clubs: the Albion, Amigos, the Arlington, the Bronx, Call the Office, the Cameron, the Club, the Commodore, Crocks 'n' Rolls, the Diamond, the Flamingo, the F.O.E., Le Foufoun Electrique, the Horseshoe, John Barley's, Luv-a-fair, the New York Theatre, the Oddfellows Hall, the O-Zone, the Power Plant, the Railway Club, the Republik, the Savoy, the Siboney, the Smilin' Buddha, the Spectrum, the Town Pump, Le Tycoon, Ultrasound, the Venue, the Westward, Wilders, Zaphods, and all the loogans who ever pogoed, stage-dove and/or drank a beer full of cigarette butts.

Those behind the scenes: Audio Plus, Cattle Prod, CBC, CFRO, Bruce Charlap, CITR, Lincoln Clarkes, Miles Constable, Chris Cran, Gary Cristall, Chris Crud, Greg Curtis, Chris Dafoe, Sherri Decembrini, *Discorder*, the Einstein Bros., Richard Flohill, Gangland, Ted Herman, Elliot L., Bud Luxford, Grant McDonough, Laurie Mercer, MoDaMu, the North Bay Steves, Jay O'Keefe, Quintessence Records, Greg Reely, Tony Ricci, John Ruskin, Cherie Sinclair, Kevin Statham, Jeff Stillie, Jerry Stoll and Teamworks.

The structure I hate also hates me, but it makes me, and that's where the problem starts

—Jeff Derksen, *Dwell*

"I have got to get this skiff. I'm getting on in years."
Miranda said without challenge, "I wish I could understand."
"It's the only thing I can do half right. It's as simple as that."
—Thomas McGuane, *Ninety-Two in the Shade*

Ladies and Gentlemen . . .

Joe Dick

March 11

Mr. Joe Dick,

My name is Laura Cromartie and I am writing to you for two reasons: 1) because you don't have a telephone; and 2) because I am wondering whether your band, Hard Core Logo, would consider doing a reunion show in order to raise money for the Green World Coalition.

The G.W.C. was formed two months ago with the intent of furthering global awareness through aggressive recycling campaigns. The benefit in question will be held on April 30 at the Arlington Cabaret and your band will be paid the sum of $800. Production is included.

If you would like more information on the G.W.C. or the benefit show, please don't hesitate to contact me. We don't have much time and there is still a considerable amount of work to be done. I was a big H.C.L. fan at university, and I would be really excited if you could help us out.

Sincerely,

Laura Cromartie

LADIES AND GENTLEMEN ...
JOE DICK

My name is Joe Dick.
I formed the seminal punk band
Hard Core Logo
back in 1977.
I was eighteen years old.
It was my ninth band.

I am now thirty-two.
The band is defunct.
It was a friendly ending,
but we played up the dissent thing
'cause that's what people wanted.

We were *the* populist band.
We manufactured our ending
to fit the mold.
That was the most commercial thing
we ever did, breaking up.

BILLY TALLENT, JOE'S OLDEST FRIEND

Billy Tallent is my oldest friend.
He is by no means my best friend.
We met in kindergarten,
and right from the start
we got in a fight:
he cut my lip
with a conductor's baton.

We were the only two in high school
who knew how to play guitar.
We'd just turned thirteen
when we formed our first band,
Peckerhead.
It lasted five minutes.
We've never played music
without one another.

JOE PHONES BILLY

You've reached 227- 4040. I've gone down to the dump to shoot rats, but I'll be back around five. Leave a message after the cool lick:

Yah, Billy, J.D. here. Listen, I'm wonderin' whether you're interested in getting Hard Core Logo together for a jam. There's this benefit thing comin' up and we could probably make a couple of hundred bucks apiece.

BILLY GETS THE MESSAGE

*What have I done since the band's broken up? Gotten depressed?
Sure. Do I drink more? Yep. Am I happier? Not as happy as I
thought I'd be.*

*What am I doing about it? Making demos of guitar feedback.
Going to Seattle to audition for bands. Looking for a woman
who'll understand me.*

*What can I do about it? Join a cover band and get off welfare?
Take a trip to the detox centre? Let Joe Dick blame me for ruin-
ing his life?*

JOE'S OLD WOUNDS

I have ninety percent hearing
in my right ear,
ten percent in my left.
I have two vocal nodes
that are inoperable.
People are always telling me
that I'm too loud, that I shout.
Half the time I can't even hear
what the hell I'm saying.

It's a conundrum, really.
The more your hearing goes,
the louder you become.
And the louder you become,
the more strain you put
on the vocal.
If the strain goes untrained
you get nodes on your throat.
Overgrown nodes cause complete
loss of voice.

BILLY PHONES JOHN OXENBURGER

Hi. I can't come to the phone right now. If you leave a message, I'll call you back as soon as possible.

Hey John-O! Billy here. Long time no talk to. Yah. Did you get a call from Joe about some benefit thing? Hmmmm. I don't know, man. Call me back, will ya? I'm still living at the same number.

JOHN GETS THE MESSAGE

The last time we broke up I felt this huge sense of relief. We had accomplished everything we possibly could; and anything else would have been, like, diminishing returns. But this feeling of relief wasn't a sustained one.

Three months after the breakup, which was the longest we'd gone without reuniting, I began going through withdrawal. My job at Canfisco was like a ball and chain. My girlfriend left me 'cause I didn't care. And, for a week or two, I'd even considered suicide.

I guess it was the way we ended it. After our last show in Toronto our road manager called us into his hotel room, one at a time, gave us our money, then split. Nobody was speaking to anyone anymore, even though we all flew back to Vancouver on the same flight. It just didn't end right.

PIPEFITTER PHONES BILLY

You've reached 227-4040. I've gone down to the dump to shoot rats, but I'll be back around five. Leave a message after the cool lick:

Dumb message, Billy. Yah, I was talkin' to John about this benefit thing and the next thing I know I'm walking down Main and I see this poster for the gig already: Hard Core Logo at the Arlington. What the fuck's goin' on? I thought we buried this band two years ago?

THE GREEN WORLD COALITION
presents

HARD ACOUSTIC REUNION!

CORE

LOGO BENEFIT

The Arlington Cabaret

APRIL 30

NO MINORS

PIPEFITTER GETS THE MESSAGE

*I need money. My clutch is broken. My only means of income is
hauling away other people's garbage; and if my truck isn't working, I'm not making any money. So I need money.*

*In the twelve years we were together we made okay money. I
never really had to work during those years, even though I knew
I'd have to get into something when it all ended. When it did end
we each got a big chunk of dough from the farewell tours. That's
when I got the notion to buy a truck.*

*Things have been pretty slow lately. Partly the economy, partly
my own laziness. It used to be fun chucking old chairs and tree
branches into the truck all day, then driving off to the dump. But
I'm not as energetic as I used to be, so I'm not taking as many
jobs. I guess I should be, though. I need the money.*

BILLY GOES OVER TO JOE'S PLACE

So I talked to the band.
Let's fuckin' do it!

T W O

First Rehearsal

FIRST REHEARSAL

If we do this
it's gonna have to be different—
no Marshalls, no bass cabs, nothing loud.
I wanna do this completely acoustic.
Pipe can play snare. John, the stand-up.

I mean it, Billy.
All those years cranked at ten,
I can't even hear the doorbell anymore.

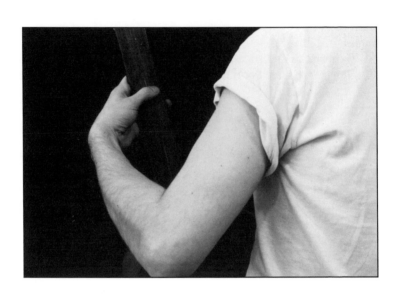

OXENBURGER'S BASS

I've got this busted stand-up.
Paid fifty bucks for it.
Never played one before.
So what I'm going to do
is colour code the fret board
like the Clash did for Simonon.

Went looking for strings last week.
A brand new set'll cost me
twice what I paid for the bass.
I'll also need a pick-up.
That's another two-fifty.

The woman I bought it from
got it from her husband.
He was a bassist for the TSO.
Played there twelve years,
then ran off with a cellist.

LOW VOLUME BILLY

This is stupid. Acoustic guitars, a stand-up bass, Pipe just playing a snare drum. Everything about this band had to do with being loud. You take away the volume, you have nothing.

JOE CALLS OUT THE SONGS

Let's start with "The Bootlegger Song."
Instead of the feedback intro
maybe Pipe you'll do one of those
rut tut-tut tut-ta things.

Rut tut-tut tut-ta . . .

THE BOOTLEGGER SONG
(FOUR O'CLOCK IN THE MORNING)

He's a crazy man with no front teeth
Lives in the basement down the street
He's got yer beer and a bottle of Screech
At four o'clock in the morning

You can see him out in the afternoon
Having breakfast at a greasy spoon
He doesn't say one word to you
'til four o'clock in the morning

    It's time to go to the ol' bootlegger
    I'm getting drunk and I want to go later
    Fifty bucks and I'll owe you a favour
    If you get me a bottle from the ol' bootlegger
    A bottle of Screech from the ol' bootlegger

He's got to be at least sixty-five
He's been selling booze since '49
He goes by the name of Mud-In-Your-Eye
At four o'clock in the morning

His room is full of pregnant cats,
Dried up food, and kerosene lamps
The smell will knock you on your ass
At four o'clock in the morning

He'll offer you a plug of chew
Then chase a cat from a tin spitoon
He'll try and tell you what's good for you
At four o'clock in the morning

But just one thing now before you go
He's got a .38 pistol that he wears down low
If you rip him off he'll let you know
At four o'clock in the morning

JOHN GOES, YAH!

This is essential Hard Core Logo! I love it! You can finally hear the words! People are finally gonna know what this band is all about! I'm getting a really good feeling about this. Now if we can just learn the songs again.

A NEW TUNE FROM JOE

I've got this new tune.
It's about Robert Satiacum.
I noticed he died the other day
at the cop shop on Powell,
just down the street.
The papers made a big deal
out of his last charge.
Child molestation.
But he was responsible
for a lot of good things, too.

A-one-two-three-four . . .

LET'S BREAK ROBERT OUT OF JAIL

He's been victimized all his life
Trying to serve his nation
The F.B.I. called him a crook
While Nixon planned a break-in

> Let's break Robert out of jail
> Let's break Robert out of jail
> Now's the time to tell the tale
> Let's break Robert out of jail

He paid no tax on his cigarettes
'cause tobacco was related
To the labour of the indigene
That the Old World had invaded

We granted him an amnesty
And our country proved safe haven
There was no way to extradite
The native of all natives

But soon enough a case was made
That he was a child molester
And when he answered to his charge
We let him die in a remand centre

PIPE DOESN'T GET IT

What the hell was that all about? Who's gonna give a shit about an Indian dying in some lock-up? I hope Joe doesn't have any-more new songs.

FOLK SONGS WE CAN COVER

The Preacher and the Slave
Give Me That Old Time Religion
Union Maid
Sail Away, Ladies
The Death of Mother Jones
Black is the Colour of My True Love's Hair
The Man that Waters the Worker's Beer
Four Nights Drunk
John Henry
I've Been Working on the Railroad
Die Gedanker Sing Frei
The Great Speckled Bird
Hold the Fort
House of the Rising Sun

MORE HARD CORE LOGO SONGS WE CAN DO

Rock 'n' Roll is Fat and Ugly
Who the Hell Do You Think You Are?
Something's Gonna Die Tonight
The Big Bush Party After School
Edmonton Block-Heater
Words and Music
Son-of-a-Bitch to the Core

SON-OF-A-BITCH TO THE CORE

Well I dig no ditch for the capitalist
I don't give change to the poor
When I throw a punch I never miss
And I'll boot your ass out the door

I've got no ties to the police line
The cops don't bug me no more
I'm a real bad ass with a bottle of wine
Yes a son-of-a-bitch to the core
Yes a son-of-a-bitch to the core

> So get off my back you business suit
> I'll pay no tax to your recruits
> If you take me on you're gonna lose
> 'cause I'm a son-of-a-bitch to the core
> Yes a son-of-a-bitch to the core

I've got a girl named Eleanor Pearl
She's the daughter of my dead wife, Jane
She's got a grin and a great big curl
But the rest of her looks pretty plain

We go to church on Something and First
Right next to the liquor store
The minister says as a dad I'm the worst
Just a son-of-a-bitch to the core
Yes a son-of-a-bitch to the core

When I get home I sit down alone
'cause Eleanor lives next door
Everyone says that I'm bad to the bone
That I'll never get up off the floor

Well what do I care if life ain't fair
If you look at me real sore

I've paid my dues and you should, too
As a son-of-a-bitch to the core
Yes a son-of-a-bitch to the core

THREE

For Immediate Release

FOR IMMEDIATE RELEASE

The Green World Coalition is pleased to present an all-acoustic reunion show by Vancouver's own Hard Core Logo. The show will be held at the Arlington Cabaret on April 30 at 8:30 p.m. Tickets are fifteen dollars and will be available at the door. All proceeds will go towards the Green World Coalition's recycling campaign. For more information please contact Laura Cromartie at 672-1963.

COPY THAT DIDN'T MAKE
THE GEORGIA STRAIGHT

Finally, from the band that threatened to kill each other and change the world in the process. Surprise. Another reunion gig. Hard Core Logo will reunite for a one hour acoustic set on April 30 at the Arlington Cabaret. Profits will go to the Green World Coalition, a newly formed organization that aims to promote peace through recycling. Should be interesting.

STAGE MANAGER/MASTER OF CEREMONIES

You must be Joe Dick?
My name is Rainbow Trout.
I will be hosting the show tonight.
Your dressing room is behind the stage.
I'm sorry I couldn't comply
with your request for imported beer.
None of the beer on your list
was politically correct enough.
I have, however, arranged for your band
to be supplied with soy beer,
compliments of the Nature's Whey corporation.

PIPEFITTER REMEMBERS

I hate hippies, man.
Everytime we've done a gig
for hippies
something bad happens.
Remember the gig on Texada?
Didn't we get burned on that one?
Didn't we get paid in pot
and busted as we drove off the ferry?

CAN I HAVE YOUR ATTENTION, PLEASE?

Put your lovin' hands together
and welcome Vancouver's favorite
bad boys of punk rock . . .

. . . the once indomitable . . .

. . . now un-top-able . . .

. . . Hard . . . Key . . . Largooooh . . .

ROCK 'N' ROLL IS FAT AND UGLY

Saturday night and I went downtown
To see a rock 'n' roll band at the Commodore
I waited in line to pay ten bucks
To see a shitty band from New York, New York
Playin' their hit from 1964

Well everyone there weighed a thousand pounds
And I was the youngest one in the crowd
Women at the bar puttin' on their make-up
Well I don't know what all the fuss is about
But rock 'n' roll is fat and ugly

I talked to a guy in a black toupee
He's a rebel all night and a lawyer by day
He went to the bar and bought me a beer
He said, C'mon let's drink! Ah, what do you say?
If I was you I'd do the same

And I talked to a woman from Florida
She was married to the guy playing lead guitar
She drove up north for her alimony
And she brought her kids; they were out in the car
Ah rock 'n' roll is sad and lonely

    Hey little boy
    Hey little girl
    Do you wanna grow up
    In a world where rock 'n' roll's
    Misunderstanding?

Well I couldn't bear just another song
Yah I tried to dance but the beat was wrong
I took a walk to the other side of town
And I ended up at an orphanage
A light was on but there was no sound

I went to the window and what did I see
Two little children dancing cheek-to-cheek
They carried the tune somewhere inside them
Yah they didn't need music for company
Ah rock 'n' roll should be so lucky

GREETINGS FROM CENTER STAGE

How the fuck are ya out there?!
Y'all been stayin' outta trouble?!
Bullshit!
I've seen you all on Robson Street,
buyin' expensive clothes
at boutiques like Ralph Lauren.
I've seen you in your bedrooms,
gettin' all dressed up
for some Socred party fundraiser.
And I've seen the way you think
the poor are so fucking romantic,
as you climb back in your limo
after an evening at *Les Mis*.
Who the hell do you think you are?
Who the hell do you think you are, anyway?

WHO THE HELL DO YOU THINK YOU ARE?

Out for dinner at Chez Henri
Who the hell do you think you are?
Rude to the waiter 'cause he looks like me
Who the hell do you think you are?

Tip the valet to get your Rolls
Who the hell do you think you are?
Take a hooker to Cypress Bowl
Who the hell do you think you are?

>Who the hell do you think you are?
>Who the hell do you think you are?

Get back home at a quarter to ten
Who the hell do you think you are?
Your wife and kids are all in bed
Who the hell do you think you are?

Pour yourself a glass of port
Who the hell do you think you are?
Pour yourself another quart
Who the hell do you think you are?

Sleep all day 'cause you're stinking rich
Who the hell do you think you are?
Call your wife a fuckin' bitch
Who the hell do you think you are?

Watch her leave 'cause she hates your guts
Who the hell do you think you are?
You thank her very, very much
Who the hell do you think you are?

PLUGGING THE RAILWAY CLUB

This next song is the last song.
It's an old folk song
and we've fucked with it
to make it new again.
It's about that little club
on Dunsmuir Street,
where we all like to go to get tanked.
A place where the working stiff
can still afford to buy a drink.
Anyone caught not singing along
will get stomped by the drummer.

I'VE BEEN DRINKING AT THE RAILWAY

I've been drinking at the Railway
All the live long day
I've been drinking at the Railway
Just to watch the Hard Cores play
Can't you hear the drinkers drinking
Rickard's Redder than your eye
Can't you hear the drinkers drinking
'til the day they die
Have another beer
Have another beer
Have another beer or two or three
Have another beer
Have another beer
Have another beer on me
Someone's in the kitchen with Billy
Someone's in the kitchen I know-oh-oh-oh
Someone's in the kitchen with Billy
#&$! %#&$!* #&%*$! %#!&$!

BILLY, AFTER EIGHT BEERS

That wasn't so bad. Kinda like playin' round a campfire. All those young girls dancing. Kinda like nymphs in a forest. Didn't feel so bad after seeing that.

By Joe's Calculations

THE POST-SHOW INTERVIEW

INTERVIEWER: Why did Hard Core Logo break up?

JOE DICK: Because we didn't get along anymore—musically speaking.

I: Just musically?

JD: Yah.

I: Well, if you had musical differences why didn't you go on to different musical projects?

JD: Because we were sick of the music business. Next question.

I: Well, why are you getting back together?

JD: Because that's what the people want. Look, we've made a few mistakes; but now we're a fuck of a lot smarter, and we want the opportunity to go out and prove it. Plus it's a whole new thing. We're going acoustic. That's the way the music was played in the thirties, when some of the best music was written. People like the Carter Family, the Almanac Singers, Leadbelly . . .

I: Are these your current influences?

JD: Yah. Particularly the politics of Woody Guthrie and Joe Hill.

I: Who is Joe Hill?

JD: Joe Hill was a member of the International Workers of the World. He was a musician and an organizer. A great man.

I: I heard Joan Baez sing a song about Joe Hill on my parents' Woodstock album. Is that the same Joe Hill?

JD: Yah. He was framed for murder by the state of Utah. They executed him in Salt Lake City around 1915.

I: What have you been doing since the break-up?

JD: I've been watching a lot of TV.

I: Anything in particular?

JD: CNN. I'm a bit of a news junkie.

I: You've written some new songs, too. Your set tonight had a new song I've never heard before, the one about Robert Satiacum.

JD: Yah.

I: Why did you write a song about Robert Satiacum?

JD: Because I believe in him.

I: Didn't he do time for child molesting?

JD: He was never convicted of child molesting.

I: What is it that you believe in, then?

JD: Robert Satiacum stood for Native Indian self-determination. I believe in that.

I: Does this mean that the new Hard Core Logo will be engaging in new political causes?

JD: There is no *new* Hard Core Logo.

I: Getting back to my first question. Last fall I read an interview in a Seattle magazine with Ed Festus, your old manager.

JD: Ex-manager.

I: Ex-manager. He said Hard Core Logo broke up because you and Billy fought all the time.

JD: Yah. But like I said the differences were musical. Musical disputes are good for a band.

I: Festus also said that you tried to kill Billy at a show in Toronto. Apparently Billy flushed something of yours down the toilet . . .

JD: That's not true. We've known each other since we were kids. We've always wrestled around and stuff and sometimes it gets heavy, but it isn't. It never is. And it wasn't about anything going down the toilet.

I: Do you think the punk rock movement was/is male-dominated? Or more specifically, do you think that one of the things the punk rock movement never aspired to was the restructuring of the male-dominated music industry?

JD: What?

I: Do you think punk rock is a boys club?

JD: No.

I: Why?

JD: Well, there were women around. Look at Nina Hagen or Wendy O. Williams. And Exene Cervenka from X.

I: Is that it?

JD: Well, I can't think of anymore right now. It's not like the women of punk rock are always on my mind.

I: What about your old label, Gilt Lick Records? Gilt Lick was one of the bigger independent labels, like SST or Slash, and they had no women in decision-making positions. Moreover, none of the widely-promoted bands on their roster are/were led by women.

JD: I don't know if that's true or what. Seems like most women artists who emerged in the late-seventies were sucked into the New Wave thing.

I: That's not necessarily true.

JD: I know.

I: Some of the local newspapers claimed that you guys sold out big time at the end, that your last year as a band was geared at making as much money as possible.

JD: Yah, well, I guess they have to write about something.

I: On paper it looks like you guys *did* sell out.

JD: Look, we'd been getting burned for years by bootleggers and bad management. We'd been working for twelve years and none of us ever had a cent. The last year was supposed to provide us with enough to last us through the years before we'd get into something else, to make a living there.

I: Didn't that go against your ideals?

JD: Like what?

I: Like mounting three final tours of Canada? Like licensing a live album to a major label? Like . . .

JD: I see nothing wrong with that. I mean, that's what the people wanted.

I: Yes, exactly. You started out with an ideal. You set out to spread the word, but you couldn't control how people would interpret your message. And that message eventually became diluted proportionate to your growing following. So at the end of it you had thousands of fans with a hackneyed view of what you were all about. And where you sold out was when you began to pander to the hackneyed view that your fans created.

JD: (shrugs) You do what you have to do, I guess.

I: There are a lot of people who read the magazine I'm submitting this interview to who were too young to remember when Hard Core Logo was just another band from Vancouver. Could you describe your beginnings? Maybe your first gig or something?

JD: Our first gig as Hard Core Logo was at the old American Hotel on Main Street. That was 1977. The place was full of bikers and transsexuals and drug addicts . . . and then we walk in with crew cuts, army boots, and ripped t-shirts. Ha! Ha! Ha! We got the gig through a guy named Mace. His real name was something like Jerry Macy; but he adopted 'Mace' 'cause it made him sound tough even though he wasn't. Anyway Mace was a friend of Billy's older brother, and he offered us a hundred bucks to open for one of his Steppenwolf-like cover bands. So there we were, hangin' by the backstage door 'cause we were under-aged and scared shitless. There was this huge biker sittin' front-and-centre starin' at us, punchin' his fist into his open hand like this (Joe demonstrates). Looking back I think he was hired by Mace just to flip us out. Ha! Ha! Ha! We had twelve songs on our set list and we figured it would cover the forty-five minutes we were supposed to be playing. Anyway we burned through the set without a pause, figuring that if we stopped they'd have a chance to beat us up. We played so fast we finished the set in thirty minutes. Everyone was speechless. It was the first punk rock gig in Vancouver. Mace was standing by the side of the stage waving his arms, going, Keep playin', keep playin'. But we didn't have anymore songs. Billy started into "Proud Mary" and we jammed on that 'til Mace had to literally drag us from the stage. The crowd was goin' nuts. They loved it. And that biker from the front table! Man! He came backstage with amyl nitrates for everybody. Ha! Ha! Ha!

I: What's next for Hard Core Logo?

JD: That'll be up to the rest of the band.

I: What do you mean by that?

JD: I don't know yet.

RETRACTION OR TRACTION

Joe Dick here.
Listen, I did an interview
with one of your reporters
and I don't want it printed.
If I find that you or any other rag
prints this interview,
I'll personally kick the shit
out of your entire staff
and sue your butts to the wall.

CALLING THE AGENT DAVE

Hey, Dave, how ya doin'?
Joe Dick here from Hard Core Logo.
Yah!
Look, man, I'm gettin' the band together.
Gettin' the itch back, ya know.
Heh-heh.
Anyway, I was thinkin' maybe
we could tour out west.
Winnipeg and back.
No. No. It's a different thing.
We're going acoustic.

I've been listening to old records.
Learning songs like "Hold the Fort"
and "New River Train,"
but doin' 'em hard and fast
like the old days.
Yah!
So what do ya say?

Nothin'?
There's got to be somethin'!
Ah, c'mon, man,
you've done well off us before.
I mean, that's got to be worth *somethin'*, right?
Yah, but Dave . . .
Dave . . .
Dave, you've been doin' what you're doin'
'cause you did so well off us
in the 1980s.
Ah, c'mon, man, that's fucked.
Yah?!
Yah?!
Well, fuck you, too!

BRUCE McROBERTS AND ASSOCIATES

Bruce?
Joe Dick here.

Yah!
Listen, I was wondering
if you'd do agency
for Hard Core Logo
out west?

Uh-huh.
Uh-huh.

So you *were* at the benefit.

Well, thanks, Bruce.
Yah, we had a great time.
In fact, we had so much fun
we want to do Winnipeg
and back.

Opening for who?
Huevos Rancheros?
What the fuck is a Huevos Rancheros?
Yah?
Uh-huh.
Ah, c'mon, Bruce.
Are you trying to get back at me
for doin' somethin' I don't remember doin'?
What do you mean you talked to Dave?
Who gives a fuck what Dave says?!
Yah?!
Yah?!
Well, fuck you too, Bruce!

BRUCE McROBERTS LEAVES A MESSAGE

You've reached 270-4040. I've gone down to the dump to shoot rats, but I'll be back around five. Leave a message after the cool lick:

Okay, you assholes, the only reason I'll book you is to piss off Dave Alfelmer. Your tour looks like this: May 13 at the Westward in Calgary; May 14 at the Club in Regina; May 15 at the Spectrum in Winnipeg; May 16 at Amigos in Saskatoon; May 17 at the Power Plant in Edmonton is tentative; and so is May 19 at the Town Pump in Vancouver. Total grosses are between $5,000 and $6,200. Production is included, so you won't need a soundman. Deposits total $800. The agency commission is fifteen percent. That's the best I can do with the shit that you guys . . . .

WELL, BILLY?

Whoa! I agreed to a reunion gig—but a tour? Hmmmm, the show did go fairly well, people definitely got into it. And Joe, he definitely had a good time. It was good to see him scowling again.

But what if I don't do this? I mean, everybody would look at me like an asshole for quitting. Or worse yet, they'd replace me with some hack and make it look like I was fired. Fuck, I don't know.

And what about Seattle? There was that last band I auditioned for. What if they call me while I'm out on the road? They could be ready to do something and I'd miss out. It could be my last chance. Ah, but it was good to see ol' Joe scowling again.

BILLY GOES OVER TO JOE'S PLACE AGAIN

Got a call from McRoberts.
He left a tour schedule
on my answering machine.
Calgary, Regina, Winnipeg,
Saskatoon, Edmonton, Vancouver.
All for small money.

Was this your idea?
I dunno, Joe.
Remember the last tour?
Lee's Palace?
If we do this
it's gonna have to be different:
no hard drugs on gig days, okay?
And it's not just me, Joe.
Pipe and John'll feel the same way.

AND JOHN?

Our show at the Arlington was one of our all-time best. If only we'd always played like that! Man, it would have been great. I'd love to have had that show every night during the farewell tours.

Joe seems clean. But then again he always seemed clean when there's talk of a tour. Last time out he was constantly stoned. Constantly. Every show got worse and worse. If Joe stayed clean and Billy stopped drinking, this tour could really fly.

Yah, I really wanna do this now. I wanna get that shitty taste out of my mouth. I wanna be able to walk off stage and feel proud again. I wanna get out there and show this country how fuckin' good a band we really were.

JOE REMINISCES

Used to be
when we were famous,
at the peak of our fame,
we'd sell a hundred t-shirts a night.
At fifteen a shirt that'd add up.
Course those were the days
when we managed ourselves.

Used to book our own tours, too.
We'd get two grand a show
and the best of hotel rooms.
Unlimited beer on the rider.
A guy to do our driving.

Our albums never sold that well.
Nothing ever got near gold.
We blame that on management.
Everything we did ourselves
always turned a profit.

PIPE?

*Almost two thousand dollars each for a week's worth of gigs.
And all I have to bring is a snare drum. Sounds good to me. I'd
have to work 150 hours at garbage removal to make the same
amount of money.*

And just think of what I could do with two thousand dollars.

*I could finally buy my neighbour's Norton. And that fly-fishing
rod in the* Buy 'n' Sell. *I could even afford to finalize my divorce.
Two thousand dollars for a week's worth of gigs. Sounds good to
me.*

SOLD TO: Joe Dick   Hard Core Logo

No phone

Date: May 4th	Prov. Sales Tax # 7%	Terms	Salesperson

QUANTITY	DESCRIPTION	LENGTH	UNIT PRICE	AMOUNT
500	Herd It Through The Bovine	C-60	$3.91	$1955.00
	Returned 1 Dat Master.			
	Paid Cash.			

**INVOICE
4415**

SUB.TOTAL	$1995.00
GST#112257332	$135.45
PROV. SALES TAX	$156.40
TOTAL	$2247.25
DEPOSIT	0
BALANCE	$2247.25

May 6th, 19 92

Received from
Reçu de   Joe Dick (Hard Core Logo)

Eighteen Hundred and Thirty —————— Dollars

200 Black T-Shirts, One Colour, One Side
including set-up, P.S.T., G.S.T
paid balance in cash

$

VAN RENTALS

The rates are as follows:

A fifteen-seat Ford van
at Cana Rentals in Richmond
is sixty dollars a day,
twenty dollars for insurance,
and five cents per k
after five hundred for free.

The same van
at Brown Brothers Ford
is seventy-five dollars a day,
twenty dollars for insurance,
and ten cents per k
after the first one thousand.

But I know a guy
who manages bands
who'll rent us his van
for fifty a day
if we fix the back wheel
and he'll give us the tire to do it.

BY JOE'S CALCULATIONS

CONCERTS

grosses:			$5000	$6200
commissions:			$ 750	$ 930
net			$4250	$5270

MERCHANDISE

grosses: (t-shirts)	200 x $20:	$4000	
(tapes)	500 x $10:	$5000	
			$9000

costs: (t-shirts)	200 x $9.15:	$1830	
(tapes)	500 x $4.50:	$2250	
			- $4080
net			$4920

MISC

van rental:	$ 300
gas:	$ 600
per diem: $20 x 4 days x 4 people:	$ 320
	$1220

concert proceeds:	$4250	$5270
merchandise proceeds:	+ $4920	+$4920
	$9170	$10190
less misc. expenses:	- $1220	- $1220
potential profit	$7950	$8970

Il Presidente
at the Wheel

JOHN'S TOUR DIARY

May 13 (a.m.)

Here we go again.

Joe insisted we leave at five a.m. on gig day in order to avoid buying hotel rooms the night before. So be it. Then he shows up at seven anyway. Pipe, as usual, is riding shotgun, bitching about how tired he is. Billy's asleep on the back bench.

We stopped for breakfast at the Petro-Can in Kamloops. Pipe, who had fallen asleep with his mouth open, remained in the van. Billy sat by himself at the coffee bar, reading *True Detective*, flirting with the waitresses. Joe and I occupied a booth by the window, watching the tourists gawk at Pipe's gaping mouth. Jeanne C. Riley was being featured on a radio program.

Joe was convinced that the cassette we were selling, entitled *Herd it Through the Bovine*, was the best thing we've done in five years—even though it was recorded live on a Sony at the Arlington. I told him I hadn't even heard it yet. He produced a copy from his Mac. The cover was hand-drawn and child-like. There was a sad looking cow in the middle, taking a dump. It looked like a bootleg.

Pipe woke up five minutes out of Kamloops, complaining of an intense hunger. Joe refused to stop until we needed gas again. Pipe then threatened to piss all over the van unless we did. Billy started siding with Pipe, and the two of them began to ride Joe. Pipe had his prick out, screaming, "It's gonna blow! It's gonna blow!" After twenty minutes they calmed down and we drove in silence. Five miles after that Joe pulled over at a fruit stand.

AT A PAY PHONE NEAR SORRENTO

Hello.
This is Joe Dick
from Hard Core Logo,
and we're playin'
the club tonight.
Could you tell me
what time's sound-check?

Yah. I'll hold.

Hello.
This is Joe Dick
from Hard Core Logo,
and we're playin'
the club tonight.
Could you tell me
what time's sound-check?

Five o'clock?

Well, we're gonna be late.
We're just east of Kamloops.
Yah.
Seven?
Okay, we'll boot it
for seven.

THE SONG ON JOE'S LIPS:
THE BIG BUSH PARTY AFTER SCHOOL

It's a Canadian tradition
When your father goes a-fishin'
And your mother goes to see her sister, too

When you have the whole gang over
'Cause the weather's gettin' warmer
Headin' out for the big bush party after school

You buy a two-four from your brother
Then again you buy another
'cause you never know who won't show up with brew

And your best friend drives a four-by
So he fills it up with ten guys
Headin' out for the big bush party after school

    It's away up the river
    It's away down the mountain
    It's away, far away as you can see
    Where the talk is never quiet
    Where the bonfire burns the brightest
    It's away, far away as you can be

So you get the fire started
And your hair is nicely parted
As you wait around for pretty Peggy-Sue

But by twelve o'clock you're loaded
And you know that she ain't showin'
Headin' out for the big bush party after school

When the weather starts a-changin'
And you've had your graduation
And you're packin' up to try on somethin' new

Take a look around your shoulder
Little sister's gettin' older
Headin' out for the big bush party after school

FROM THE SHOTGUN POSITION

Check it out, man!
A skinhead hitchin'—
in Revelstoke!
Let's pick him up.

THE SKINHEAD LASTS A MILE

Hard Core Logo?
Never heard of you.

LUNCH AT THE GOLDEN ARMS
MOTOR HOTEL

Okay.

One double burger.
No lettuce, tomatoes,
or mayo.
Side of onion rings.
Diet-coke.

Chicken pie.
Side house salad.
Strawberry Jello.
Decaf.

Spaghetti and meatballs.
Garlic toast.
Chocolate shake.
Cheesecake.

Chef's salad
Clam chowder.
Corn bread.
Postum.

ONE OF BILLY'S GIRLS

Had a girlfriend from Golden.
She was Miss Golden of something.
Came down to Vancouver
for the PNE pageant
and lost.
Badly.
Applied as a model,
but never got called.
Got a job at McDonald's,
then quit to go stripping.

I met her one summer
at the A-2 Café.
She was working the Five
right down the street.
Just the two of us talking,
laughing at dreams.

IL PRESIDENTE AT THE WHEEL

We've been making good time.
Should be in Calgary
eight o'clock Mountain.

The contract says two sets,
forty-five minutes apiece.
We'll do an hour-ten.

Pipe, you load us in.
Billy, you tune the strings.
John, draw up a stage plot.

LOCAL No. 145

AMERICAN FEDERATION OF MUSICIANS OF THE UNITED STATES AND CANADA
(hereinafter called American Federation of Musicians)

CA1

CONTRACT FOR CANADA

THIS CONTRACT for the personal services of musicians, made this ..8th. day of .....May........................ 19.....

between the undersigned purchaser (hereinafter called the "Purchaser") and .... 4 .... musicians (hereinafter called
(Including Leader)
"Musicians") represented by the undersigned Representative;

WITNESSETH THAT the Purchaser contracts for the personal services of the Musicians, as musicians severally, and the Musicians
severally, through their Representative, agree to render collectively to the Purchaser services as musicians in the orchestra/band under the
leadership of ....Joe..Mulgrew/Hard..Core..Logo........................ according to the following terms and conditions:

Place of engagement: ....The..Westward..Hotel....................................

Date(s) of engagement: ....May..13,1991..............................

Hours of engagement and starting time: ..Load..in:....tba....Soundcheck:....tba......
Doors..open:..8pm....Sets:....2../..45..minutes......
Start..time:..10pm....Closing..time:..2am............

Type of engagement: (Specify whether Dance, Stage, Show, Banquet, etc.) ....Cabaret..............

Fee agreed upon: $1250.00.....plus..production,accomodations,rider,and..deposit..of..50%.
........($625.00)..payable..to..Bruce..Dubious..and..Associates..upon..receipt..of..contract.
Cap: 275   Tix: $5.00

To be paid: ......Upon..completion..of..engagement..in..CASH..ONLY..............................
(Specify when payments are to be made)

The terms and conditions set out in SCHEDULE 1 hereof are part of this contract.

Joe Mulgrew
_____   _____
Purchaser's Name   Signature of Leader

_____
Signature of Purchaser

......119-12th..Ave...S.W...Calgary,Ab.....   ....441..Powell..St...Vancouver,B.C.........
Street Address   Street Address

....
City   Province   City   Province

........(403)..265..5641.............   ....
Phone No.   Phone No.

Names of musicians.			Local Union No.	Canadian Social Insurance No. or U.S. Social Security No.	Minimum Basic Fee
Surname	Given Name	Initials			
Mulgrew	Joseph	(Leader) R	145	▒▒▒▒▒▒	
Boisy	William	W	145	▒▒▒▒▒▒	
Oliphant	John	B	145	▒▒▒▒▒▒	
Dubinsky	Ronald	Z	145	▒▒▒▒▒▒	

JOHN'S TOUR DIARY

May 13 (p.m.)

Tonight was the worst night of my life. We blew it right from
the start. Served us right, though. Joe was like the Joe of old.
Screaming at anything that didn't scream back. Should've
brought a soundman.

Sound-check was awful. Couldn't get the feed-back off my bass.
Billy kept demanding more guitar in the monitor. His soloing
volume was three times louder than our total output. I don't
know if Joe's voice is going to last the tour.

The worst part was all the people who showed up. Young kids
who'd never seen us before. I remember wanting to put my sun-
glasses on; I couldn't bare to look them in the eye. It seemed
like Joe broke a string every second song. And Pipe! Pipe does
not like playing without a full kit.

We ended the night with the worst version of "Hair" ever. We'd
never even rehearsed it, and Billy claims he never even knew
such a song existed. Still, the crowd loved it. They were going
wild. And that's what really bugged me the most.

JOE GOES OVER THE OPTIONS

It's a ten-hour trip
from here to Regina.
If we leave here tonight
and drive it in shifts
we can get our hotels
by one-thirty.
Sound-check's at six,
so a five hour nap
would give us,
all told,
our eight hours.

Or we could stay here the night
and leave at eleven,
blow out the sound-check,
and get there at tennish.
The opening band
gets off at ten-thirty,
so we could load in and play
then sleep through the morning.

SIX

Set List by Committee

JOHN'S TOUR DIARY

May 14 (a.m.)

Joe has not slept since we left Vancouver. That was thirty-two hours ago. I'm convinced he's doing blow, but no one will confront him. I tried to take the wheel in Swift Current and a pushing match ensued. Joe won out, of course. It's as if he's hauling a cross or something.

We're right on the verge of Regina. Everyone stinks of booze and stage-sweat. The van is littered with pop cans and donut icing. There's a banana peel hanging from the rear-view mirror. This is easily the worst part of the tour.

The city of Regina looks like the set from *The Last Picture Show*. Businesses boarded up, people wandering around in a daze. Regina has always been depressing. But depressed? What's going on here? What are people doing? Pipe says they're hosting the NHL awards here in June.

Tonight's gig is at the Club. We used to play the Venue, but I heard it burned down. We're staying at the Sandman Inn for the ninth consecutive time. Apparently the Sandman's got the biggest hotel swimming pool in Western Canada. Never seen it, though. Always too tired.

JOE PUTS IT INTO PERSPECTIVE

Getting people together
for a rock band
and an attitude
is like living in a co-op.
But trying to get a booking
is like sales
for small commission.

While loading up the van
makes me feel
like I'm in shipping,
it's driving to some tavern
that makes me feel
like I'm a trucker.

Setting up on stage
makes me feel
like I'm a millwright,
or a puppet
who is tangled
for a moment
during sound-check.

And lately, like a goldfish
when the stage lights
hide the public,
I work my strings
and notice
how this job's
like all the rest.

HARD CORE LOGO'S IDEAL RIDER

24 bottles of Dos Equis beer

24 bottles of domestic beer (nothing 'light')

1 mickey of Jack Daniels

4 bottles of mineral water

2 pitchers of Coca-Cola Classic

4 hot meals at sound-check

A meat-generous deli-tray to be served in the dressing room immediately after the last encore

A television set with VCR hook-up. The last half-hour of *Apocalypse Now* must be playing just before show-time

PIPE TEASES BILLY

There's a girl out there
says she knows you.

She's got a baby
at her mother's.
Says that baby
looks just like you.

I told her
that you gave up music,
that you took a job
in a laundromat.

She got upset
and wouldn't stop crying.
The younger brother
took her home.

SET LIST BY COMMITTEE

There's nobody here.
Cut out the ballads.
Throw in the fast stuff.
We'll start with the fast stuff.
We'll get them up dancing.
There's nobody here.
I hope they'll be drinking.
How much are tickets?
Did you see some promotion?
Let's start with some covers.
There's nobody here.
Who else is in town?
There's only one club.
I think it's stopped raining.
Let's wait 'til ten-thirty.
Let's wait 'til eleven.
There's nobody here.
Where's the promoter?
He's gonna lose money.
Have you seen the owner?
The owner's promoting.
He's not even here.
There's nobody here.

JOE, EYES GLAZED BY NARCOTICS, DEDICATES THE FIRST SONG

This song is defecated to all
the drug addicts and pedophiles
who dominate the music business.

WORDS AND MUSIC

You've got some words and music
You think they sound real perfect
You want to play them for your mom

The words are deeply moving
The music's very groovy
You want to play them in a club

    You meet some manager
    Who loves the way you dress
    You sign your name to his
    He promises he'll do his best for twenty percent

You make a four song demo
For the local college radio
In a week you're sittin' on the charts

Then a guy from Sick-O Records
Hears you while he's playin' checkers
And he wants to sign you on the spot

    You meet his company
    They take you out for lunch
    You sign the record deal
    They take your picture having fun ha! ha! ha!

You're off to some big city
Where they make you look real pretty
You have to thank them, though it's hard

And when they've made your album
When they've made it sound like pablum
They want to see it top the charts

    You meet the agency
    They send you town to town

You know you can't come back
Until the record sells around a million billion

But no one out there buys it
And the critics call it dog shit
And all your friends think you're uncool

Now you've got new words and music
And you know they're less than perfect
But it's good enough for what you do

MARY THE FAN

Hey John-O!
Good to see you.
Been a long time, eh?
Five years?
Wow!

Joe!
You guys sound great.
Better than ever.
That new song,
about the dead guy
in jail?
A classic.

Is that Pipe?
Last time I saw Pipe
he had a pig-shave.
I wish my hair
would grow that fast.

Oh, Billy!
Gimme a hug.
Mmmmm-mm
Oooo, honey,
how'd you get that nasty
scar on your hand?

THE SCAR ON BILLY'S PALM

I was walking home
drunk one night
when I fell
on a case of empties.

THE SCAR ON BILLY'S PALM
(JOHN'S VERSION)

Our last gig in L.A.
was at Madame Wong's on Wilshire.
The upstairs where we played was packed,
and we got eighty percent of the door.
We had three days off
before Phoenix,
so we drove all night for Baja.
We were itchin' to blow some money.

We pulled into a place called Sol,
which means sun in Spanish,
and ordered five bottles of mescal.
Man, there were whores everywhere!
And the kids! Totally pathetic.
They're supposedly maimed at birth
for careers as professional beggars.
This girl with no arms
comes up to us with a basket
attached to her chest.
And the sign above it reads:
AMERICAN DOLLARS ONLY.

Anyway, we got pissed silly.
And we were kinda weirded out,
so we got set to leave
when this guy named Hey-Zeus
walks in with this bass.
A great, big mariachi bass.
Billy sat down with it
and played "Smoke on the Water."
Hey-Zeus sold it to Billy for twenty bucks.

We finished the tour just before Christmas,
with the bass riding shotgun
all the way home.
We dropped Billy off
at his parents' in Mission;
then they had us all back
for this huge turkey dinner.
At the end of the night
Billy got the bass
to play "Silent Night"
for his nieces and nephews.
He got halfway through
when the damn thing exploded.
Unacclimatized to our weather, I guess.

PIPE DEMOS THE ENTIRE DELI-TRAY INTO ONE SANDWICH

The trick here is to work sideways.
I'm using the two Coke pitchers
as bookends as I go.

Bread, cheese, meat, bread,
lettuce, cheese, bread, pickles,
meat, bread, lettuce, cheese,
bread, cheese, meat, bread.

I guess you're wondering how
I'm gonna stand this up, right?

Bread, cheese, meat, bread,
lettuce, cheese, bread, pickles,
meat, bread, lettuce, cheese,
bread, cheese, meat, bread.

Why stand it up
when it's gonna be eaten?

Bread, cheese, meat, bread,
lettuce, cheese, bread, pickles,
meat, bread, lettuce . . .

BILLY BY THE FIRE EXIT

Touring sure has changed. I remember when there were at least a dozen girls waiting around for us backstage. It used to be a whole new show after the last encore.

Mary used to be some girl. I remember when she had purple hair and wore nothing but black leather. Now she shows up with her lawyer husband and their eight-year-old daughter.

Joe never seemed to pay much attention to the girls. He was always too busy running the show. Pipe met his ex-wife in Thunder Bay; and John spent six years with a girl he met in Montreal. I wish I kept in touch with some of the girls I met. Some of them were real nice.

JOE GETS PAID

Okay.

Twenty.
Forty.
Sixty.
Eighty.
One.

Twenty.
Forty.
Sixty.
Eighty.
Two.

Twenty.
Forty.
Sixty.
Eighty.
Three.

Four.
Five.
Six.
Seven.
Eight.
Nine.
Ten.

Great Show.

A NOTE FOR THE BAND

Hard Core Logo —
Your gig in Winnipeg
has been cancelled.
Phone Bruce for
details.

JOHN'S TOUR DIARY

May 15 (a.m.)

Just got in from a party upstairs. A bunch of kids from high school were having a pre-grad bash. Somebody was loading up cannisters with nitrous oxide, turning everyone into children again. Got out of there just in time. The cops passed me on the way down.

Tonight's show was much better than the Westward gig—despite the fact that we didn't get a sound-check. When we went on stage there were maybe twenty people in the building; but as soon as we started playing, the place filled up. We sold ninety-seven tapes and fifty-five t-shirts. That's almost three times what we did in Calgary.

Joe was furious that the Winnipeg date was cancelled, although I suspect he's relieved we don't have to travel all day and back for bad money. Joe's going to phone Bruce tomorrow and get the whole story.

Since we have the day off today, Joe suggested that we stop off on the way to Saskatoon and visit Bucky Haight. The last time we saw Bucky was five years ago at CBGB's in New York City. He had just finished producing an album that never got released. We were on our way to Boston, to a gig we never got paid for.

Bucky Got Drunk, Told Stories

JOHN'S TOUR DIARY

May 15 (a.m.) continued

I awoke to Joe screaming into the telephone. He was standing
by the window, the morning sun a spotlight to the boner in his
briefs, livid that our gig got cancelled. Joe's mad vein, the vein
running up the side of his forehead, was in full plume. This is a
bad sign. Joe's mad vein has been known to foreshadow severe
changes in the weather. I haven't seen Joe pop a mad vein since
the day Ed Festus ran off with our bank account.

Anyway, we're out of a gig. Seems like no one was interested.
How do you argue with that one? I can't say I blame people.
We seem to represent everyone's worst vices. And despite the
young blood at our Calgary show, our audience *is* getting older:
if they haven't indulged themselves to death already, then
they've probably gone on to safer things, right? I'll have to put
that one to Bucky. He'll know.

We had breakfast at a truck stop north of Lumsden. Everyone
sat together for the first time on the tour. Billy had a funny joke
about a tractor and a sheep. He got Pipe laughing so hard a
piece of bacon shot out of his nostril and landed on top of Joe's
pancakes. And Joe, instead of going nuts, ate it. So far, so good.

JOE SETS THE COURSE

A few hundred k
up #11 to Davidson.
Another forty to #19,
then twenty to Elbow.
That's where Bucky's living.
In a big, black barn
on Diefenbaker Lake.

BUCKY GOT DRUNK, TOLD STORIES

I

New York City.
When I first got there
I knew one person.
Johnny Thunders.
I knew Johnny Thunders.

A friend of his, Nate,
picked me up at the airport.
He took me by cab
to the Lower Eastside,
up two flights of stairs
to this eight-by-eight room.
He told me to wait there,
that Johnny'd be calling,
then he left me
with two hundred dollars.

The room overlooked
this alleyway.
A greasy-brown trench
where hookers checked in
with their pimp
for injections.
They'd lift up their skirts
and stick out their butts,
at the same time counting
his money.

Pieces of paint
hung from the ceiling.
A dirty green foam
covered most of the floor.
There never was a telephone.

Like, you can't take calls
if there ain't no phone,
right?

So I make for the door.
But it's locked and I'm shittin'.
Thunders, man, he set me up!
I begin to envision
the *Globe and Mail*:
CANADIAN PUNK DIES
IN NEW YORK CITY.

All of a sudden
the door flies open.
These two big dudes
in black leather jackets
toss me a baggy
of fine white powder.
They demand four hundred
and fifty-five dollars.

I only had three hundred,
so I make up the difference
with the money from Nate.
I give them the money
and they give me this card:

SEVEN PERCENT
OFF YOUR NEXT TRANSACTION

PEACE IN THE BIG HEREAFTER

I could hear their laugh
all the way outside.
I felt like such a fuckin' jerk.
Here I am in New York City
and first thing I do
is get stuck for a mark.
Another stupid tourist story.

II

I never did see Thunders.
When I began my meetings
with the record company
the mere mention of his name
brought everyone down.
And after my meetings
I got so involved
in what I was up to
that I didn't have time
for anything other
than what I was doing.

III

I signed a deal
to make an album.
A world-wide release,
then options to follow.
They advanced me a cheque
for two hundred grand
and I gave them back

1) a chunk of the publishing

2) huge points on sales

3) and all but a penny
   on t-shirts, posters,
   stickers, and buttons

When I got up to leave
they held out their hands
to say that a deal
is only as good
as the handshake it's made on.

And now, looking back, I remember
the look on the president's face
when he told me "carte blanche"
when I wanted "good luck."

IV

I've never hired management.
I've never hired a lawyer.
I'd always felt that
I'd know best when someone's
gonna rip me off.

My father had a saying once
that's crippled me for life:
"Never trust those close to you."
So no one's ever gotten close.

V

So there I was in N.Y.C.,
happy as a gnat in shit,
a ton-o-bucks in my pocket,
with no place to live,
no friends to call up,
and no idea how I was
gonna make my album.

I leased a warehouse space
just off the Hudson River,
rented a sixteen channel board,
ten mikes, a tape deck,
then checked out the clubs
for some decent musicians.

The punk rock players
were the absolute shits,
so I had this notion
to hire some jazz guys.
The two guys I hired,
the Del Rio brothers,
had a fern bar gig
near N.Y.U.
Vitto on drums, Carmine on bass.
They came from a family
of red-hot musicians;
their uncle or something
knew Brian Wilson
and did some work
on the *Pet Sounds* record.
Anyway, they sounded smart
so I advanced them two grand
to start the next day.

My engineer was a Nashville-type
who couldn't work in Nashville.
I met him at a Chris Hillman gig
and he told me the story
of how he voted McGovern
and happened to tell a few people
and the next thing he knew
he was kicked out of Nashville
and, anyway, he liked me so . . .

It's ten o'clock the next morning.
The Del Rios arrive, set up,
and my engineer, Rudy,
is ready to roll.
We decide to run each tune once,
then lay down a couple of takes;
and we did it this way
'til we finished five songs.
We took a break at four
and listened back.

VI

And it was perfect!
Exactly what I wanted.
Kind of a cross
between Mingus and the Buzzcocks.
So we ran five more
and it just got better.
I called up a limo
to take us to dinner.
Some dump in Queens
recommended by Carmine.

We ate and we drank
and took more limos
and drank more booze
and bought some good blow
and took more limos
and drank more booze
and the next thing I know
I'm waking up in Central Park
with the light in my eyes
and two guys trying
to yank off my boots.

I'd been picked over all night,
and the boots were the last
of the meat, so to speak,
off my bones.
I got up
and watched as they ran
past the nannies, the joggers,
to the edge of the park,
where they fought over who
got to take home the pair.
No money. No boots.
It's the middle of winter
and it takes me three hours
to make my way back.

And it just gets worse.
Everything in the space
had been stolen.
I phone up Rudy.
No answer.
I phone the Del Rios
and the line is busy.
I grabbed some money
I'd stashed in the closet
and hailed a cab downstairs.
I was so pissed I was shitting.
I kicked in the Del Rios' door
and the first thing I saw
was the phone off the hook;
then a melted candle,
a burnt spoon,
and the sound of a shower
by that time colder
than my bare feet.

VII

The Del Rios o.d.'ed.
Rudy was caught in New Jersey
with everything but the masters,
which he'd dumped in The Hudson.
And I was back to square one.
I'd never been that mad,
that happy, that sad,
and that scared
as I had been in less than one day.

VIII

For the next three weeks
I sat in my warehouse,
eating Kraft Dinner,
picking my nose.

IX

My first nervous breakdown.
I spent two months
in a halfway house,
and when I got out
I called up a meeting.
I told the record company
that the project was finished,
and that I needed a rest
'til I started the mixing.
They all agreed
it was a great idea.
Then they asked me
to do them
a really big favour:
to fly to L.A.
and produce them a band.

X

They had this band.
A band with no name,
no songs, no talent.
But, god, they were beautiful!
The most beautiful boys
in the world.
And they knew who I was!
They heard a bootleg
of my show in Miami
and they called A&R
to demand I produce them.

It didn't matter that they were assholes.
They wanted to make beautiful music.
Music that was soft and beautiful
played hard and ugly.
This was their idea:
Bacharach and David
turned upside down.

We spent three weeks
in a drug-induced blur.
I made a deal
with the company weasels
not to come 'round
'til the record was done.
We'd go in at five
and record off-the-floor,
cranking out tunes like
"Walk On By"
"Blue on Blue"
"What's New, Pussycat?"
"Here I Am"
downing peyote
with glasses of port.

At midnight or so we'd go out for lunch,
ordering meals we never could eat.
The boys all made sure
they got known around town;
that they were all paid
to make beautiful music,
played super-fast,
played hard and ugly.
And that I was their god;
and that I played their game
'til I woke up busted
in an Anaheim jail.

The record company made a deal:
they'd get me out
if I played them the tracks.
So I'm back in the studio
two hours later, and the engineer's
laughing his guts out.
I'm sitting with the head
of world A&R,
who's fifty years old
and a friend of the Bacharachs,
listening to punks doing
"Walk On By"
"Blue on Blue"
"What's New, Pussycat?"
"Here I Am."
And after four more,
after sitting there silent,
he picks up the phone
and holds for Hal David.
Then he covers the phone,
gives me a wink,
and tells me
they'll love it in Europe.

XI

So I'm back in New York,
hailed as hero,
and the company wants me
to handle young bands.
They postpone my album,
move me uptown,
and give me ten demos
of the bands they'd just signed.
For the next three years
I'm their hottest producer,
yet none of the records
I do get released.

By the mid-1980s
I just call it quits.
I move down to Texas
and record *Blue Tattoo*.
It's picked up in England
by a small independent
and gets credited
in circles
with starting roots-rock.
But I'm still under contract
with the big major label,
so they hand me a lawsuit
and the record's recalled.

XII

The last time you saw me, at CBGBs,
I was hyping two bills a day.
It got so bad after you left
I started needing blood transfusions.
Needless to say I couldn't work;
and what work I did was awful.
All of my friends were dead or dying.
Everyone I met sucked up to me.

I realized I had to leave
when I got that dirty needle.
I was diagnosed with hepatitis.
The very same strain as Naomi Judd.

XIII

If I could give you all
one piece of advice:
ditch the band
and buy a farm.
It doesn't matter what you grow.
It's the fact that you'll see
whatever you do.

JOHN'S TOUR DIARY

May 15 (p.m.)

The visit with Bucky was not what I expected. He lived in the loft of a modified barn, and this Native girl looked after him. I reckoned he'd be healthier, but he looked as bad as he did in the eighties. Most of the time we sat and listened, drinking his beer and eating his food. He had a way of putting things, where everything's funny and sad at once.

We drove in silence down the highway. I could tell that Joe was really bummed. While Billy and Pipe were bemused by Buck, Joe grew more despondent. Billy began an imitation: Buck's drawn out way of lighting a smoke, his pathetic attempt at flicking the ash. I could feel a storm beginning to brew, but Joe kept on driving.

EIGHT

A New Tune to Practice

JOE ON THE MIKE

Hello, Saskatooooooon!
We're Hard Core Logo.
We're gonna sing a song or two
to prepare you for tomorrow.
This one's written by Bucky Haight,
the legendary punk king
who died last year in New York City.

BLUE TATTOO

It hurt so bad when you got it
It went right to your head
It drove you insane
But now that's all forgotten
And you can go on
Without any pain

A blue tattoo on your shoulder
In the shape of a heart
In the middle of my name
And that's how I remember
All of the bad things
That you couldn't change

Blue Tattoo
Blue Tattoo

You had no time for corruption
You felt that the world
Was an unsafe place
You worked towards a solution
But the best you could do
Was to send me away

A blue tattoo on my shoulder
In the shape of the world
In the middle of your name
And that's how I remember
All of the good things
You took to your grave

Blue Tattoo
Blue Tattoo

JOHN'S TOUR DIARY

May 16 (a.m.)

Since there were no touring bands playing the club last night, and we had the whole day off, the promoter let us have the band rooms upstairs—for free. He asked us if we wanted to come down later, and maybe do a couple of songs on the open stage to hype tomorrow's show. At that point, Pipe charged into the conversation and said we'd do it for twenty bucks a song. We all laughed.

We ended up playing two half-hour sets. Originally we'd planned to play three or four songs, but the crowd was loving it. *Really* loving it. And by the end of the first set people were lining up at the telephone, trying to get their friends out to what was becoming a perfectly spontaneous event.

For the first time in a long time I began to realize how special this band was to people. I felt really proud. I felt part of something bigger than all of us. Standing there on the stage I got to thinking that maybe we were meant to stay together. Forever. And when Joe opened the night with Bucky's "Blue Tattoo," which caught us all off guard, I felt like crying.

When the doors closed, we invited the promoters and the owners upstairs for a poker party. Everybody took turns winning, and the beers were flowing freely. We were all having a good time, until Joe ruined it by insisting that the club should give us full payment for the extra show. And then Pipe started multiplying the number of songs by twenty. Nobody was laughing then.

PIPE UNDER HIS BREATH

Having a shitty time doin' this. Should have listened to my gut. Joe's an asshole. Billy's a jerk-off. John's a fuck-head.

I was led to believe I'd be making some okay money. Now it looks as though I won't even make my rent. Hell, what do you expect when you're doing gigs for free?

Bucky's lucky. He still gets royalty cheques. He doesn't have to worry about making ends meet. Plus he's got someone looking after him. Shit, I wish I was in his shoes.

BILLY ON HOLD AT THE NELSON HOTEL

*The first time Joe and I met Bucky was backstage at the Smilin'
Buddha. 1979. He was passing through town with some band
from the States, and our friend, Ed Festus, was a buddy. It was
our first ever backstage visit.*

*I never thought much of the great Bucky Haight. He was a shitty
singer, an even worse guitarist. But he managed to write some
pretty good songs. Songs only he could deliver. He's always been
a god to Joe.*

*Bucky's the reason we started this band. When I taught Joe gui-
tar I tried to get him to learn the classics—Johnson, Leadbelly,
Hendrix, Van Halen. But Joe never much got into that. He only
liked the music he knew. And the music he knew was Bucky.*

A FREELANCE INTERVIEW
AT THE WOOLWORTH'S COFFEE BAR

INTERVIEWER: I thought you guys were dead or something.

JOE DICK: We're very much alive, thank you.

I: How's the tour going?

JD: Great. All the shows have been sell-outs. We even sold out in Winnipeg, but had to cancel due to unforeseen circumstances.

I: Why did you guys decide to reunite?

JD: We decided to reunite because that's what people wanted. We've always been *the* populist band, eh? We're slaves to the people. It's what we had to do.

I: You sound like Tommy Douglas.

JD: Tommy Douglas. A great man.

I: Besides going acoustic, is there anything different about Hard Core Logo?

JD: Yes and no. (pause)

I: Can you elaborate?

JD: Well . . . what was the question again?

I: Anything *new* with Hard Core Logo?

JD: Right. Besides going acoustic we're writing again. Our song about Robert Satiacum is a smash hit.

I: Didn't he do time in Alberta for racketeering? Selling cigarettes or something?

JD: Yah, and now he's dead. He died in a Vancouver lock-up. He was charged with a crime and he died waiting for his trial. See, his heart was going and he surrendered to get medical help. He had a heart attack and the guards just watched him suffer. That's the true crime.

I: Is is true that the legendary Bucky Haight has returned to his native Saskatchewan?

JD: I don't comment on legends.

I: The last time you came through here, in '89, I had an interesting chat with your manager, Ed Festus. He was telling me that punk was gonna make a big comeback, and that he was trying to prime you guys for the nostalgia circuit.

JD: Ed Festus. That fucker!

I: Right. I understand Ed's moved on.

JD: Yah, well *we* moved him on. Fuckin' crook. We don't usually talk about Ed, but let me just say that we're suing him for stealing the rights to our name.

I: Well, how did this come about?

JD: We had some tax problems in the mid-1980s. That's when we hired Ed. He was our friend at the time, and he knew a bit about finances. Everything ended up getting transferred into his name.

I: So legally he could sue *you*? Aren't you worried about that?

JD: Are you kidding? A lawsuit would be the best thing ever to happen to us. The problem is that Ed knows that, too. If anybody else owned our name we'd be laughing.

I: So what's the problem?

JD: It's personal. It goes deeper than money.

I: I hear Ed's living in Seattle, managing grunge bands.

JD: We know exactly what he's doing. I feel sorry for the musicians signed to his company. He's probably screwing them like he did us. Look, the Ed Festus stuff is turning me off this interview.

I: Sorry.

JD: I'll allow you one more question. Better make it a good one.

I: Is there any future in what you are doing?

JD: Yes. Now fuck off.

JOE'S KEY WORDS TO A NEW SONG

Grain Tower
General store
Reduced prices
No credit

Million dollar debt
Savings and loan
Bank manager
Near the church

Poor farmer
Wheat in the donut
Feel like the chaff
Ticket punch

Bad times
Moves the family
Gives up hockey
Gives up pool

Transfer
Liar
The Reverend's opinion
Everyone's opinion

A NEW TUNE TO PRACTICE

I was having lunch
up on Broadway
and these three guys
were talking
about their fathers, farmers
up near Lloydminster.
Got most of it down
on this napkin.

THE TICKET PUNCH AT THE
SAVINGS AND LOANS

I took my grain to the tower
Across the street from the general store
I almost made enough money
For a bottle of Coke and the drive back home

I owe your bank a million dollars
And every year it's a million more
I drive by there every Sunday
On my way to church, when I know you're at home

    I am the poor farmer
    I am the road that leads to town
    I am the wheat in your donut, yes
    But I feel like the chaff when you come around
    The ticket punch at the savings and loans

I could tell bad times were a-comin'
When you moved your wife to Saskatoon
When you gave up Saturday hockey
When you stopped playin' pool at the hotel saloon

Now you're puttin' in for a transfer
'cause you're ready to move on to something new
But we all know you're a liar
And The Reverend Jim he thinks so, too
Yah The Reverend Jim he thinks so, too

JOHN'S TOUR DIARY

May 16 (p.m.)

Went downtown at 8 a.m., the earliest I've been up since we left. Had breakfast at the Nelson Hotel. Steak and eggs, toast and coffee.

Went to the Mennonite clothing store and bought a belt.

Practiced Joe's new song—in silence.

Leaving right after the gig.

A SULKING PIPE

Everytime I look at John he's writing in his fuckin' notebook. He never used to do this before. He was just like the rest of us: drinking hard and chasing women. Mind you, nobody's chasing women anymore. And Billy's the only real drinker.

Still, it picks me. But I know what he's up to. Last year I read something John wrote in Discorder: *some anonymous thing only he could have known of. It was all about the early years: Subhumans, K-Tels, gigs at the Buddha.*

I know he's writing a story on us. A tell-all thing that'll make me look stupid. There's no fucking way I'll sign a release. I'll just wait 'til it's published, then hire a lawyer.

SASKATOON MAY 16 (SET LIST)

Who The Hell
R 'n' R Is Fat
Hold The Fort
Robert
The Worker's Beer
Something's Gonna
Railway
Ticket Punch
Medly #1
Blue Tattoo
Bush Party
Block. Heater
4 Nights Drunk
Medly #2
Bootlegger Song
S.O.B.
Words And Music
_____
Proud Mary

THE BARTENDER CAUTIONS JOE

Don't get me wrong.
It's nothing personal, Joe,
but could you please tell Billy
that *our* rider agreement
specifies draught beer only?
Also, there's a six pint
limit per person,
and Billy's already
nine pints over.
And one more thing, Joe.
Could you please tell him
to lay off the waitresses?
The two on last night
have refused to come in.

JOE IGNORES THE ENCORE

The club owner wants an encore,
but there's no fuckin' way
I'm gonna go out there
and play to a crowd
of five people.

ENCORE

Thank you very much.
You've been a terrific crowd.
Joe just collapsed upstairs
from all the excitement,
so me, Pipe, and Billy
are gonna give you
our rendition
of the Safaris' classic,
"Wipeout."

Something's Gonna Die Tonight

THE FAX FROM BRUCE

Attn: Joe Dick

The Town Pump is on the verge of becoming a non-smoking, top-forty club. They're honouring some bookings, but, unfortunately, not yours.

Your Power Plant show in Edmonton has been moved to a smaller venue, the O-Zone. The promoter's putting you on a bill with a band made up of ex-Jr. Gone Wild guys. Make sure he pays you the $300 up front.

What else can I say? That's rock 'n' roll!

JOHN'S TOUR DIARY

May 17 (a.m.)

Joe got a fax from Bruce regarding our gigs at the Power Plant and the Town Pump, which have now been cancelled. Oddly enough, Joe didn't seem bothered by the cancellations. I figured he'd blow up and try to break something; but he just shrugged his shoulders and said, "Oh, well," when he told us. We're playing the O-Zone instead.

The turn-out in Saskatoon last night was pathetic. It seemed as if everyone dug the spontaneous show the night before and felt they'd had enough. I think there were nine people left when we finished. Billy said something about a grunge band blow-out downtown, so that probably accounted for the small crowd.

We ended up getting an extra $200 for our spontaneity. It was hardly worth it, though, since they probably hate our guts after the scene Joe and Pipe pulled. I doubt they'll ever have us back. But then again, I doubt we'll ever be back.

I know there's only one more show left, but I don't know how much more of this I can take. I'm sick of Billy drinking all the booze rider. And I'm sick of Pipe eating all the deli-tray. And as for Joe. . . . Well, I'm just sick of Joe.

INVENTORY

	Calgary	Regina	Saskatoon	
Tapes in total:				500
Tapes sold:	37	97	20	154
Tapes given away: *(promo)*	22	47	57	126
T-shirts in total:				200
T-shirts sold:	19	55	22	96
T-shirts given away: *(promo)*	8	11	12	31

JOE CALLS A BAND MEETING
AT THE STRATHCONA HOTEL

I've got bones to pick
and one positive thing
to say to you all.

Pipe. Your whining.
Everybody's fed up
with your attitude.
The hotel guy in Regina
phoned to say
you left a turd
on your pillow,
and that you wiped your ass
on the bedspread.
Uncool, man.
If you've got a problem
don't take it out
on the cleaning staff
or anyone else
you've never met.

John. Your writing.
You're making us
totally paranoid.
Pipe's already told me
he's gonna fight you
for your diary
or whatever it is
you're keeping from us.
So I want you to stop it
or I'll let Pipe kill you.

And Billy. Billy.
When I paid your phone bill
in Calgary I noticed
you called Ed Festus,

not once but twice.
Didn't I tell you
that he's not to be
talked to?
How many times
have you gotta be told, eh?

On the positive side
the tour's almost over.
You're all getting paid
right after the show.

Joe Dick
is
a fascist
a coke addict
and a bad driver

PIPE FEELS RIPPED OFF

I was promised almost two thousand dollars. Now Joe informs me I might make six hundred. I should've known this couldn't work. Story of my life—this couldn't work.

I never grew up with money like Joe. Even John and Billy grew up middle-class. When we first started out those guys had great gear—Gibsons and Fenders and big Marshall amps. I had the same drums I got when I started. A bright orange kit my folks bought at Sears.

Joe, John, and Billy write all the songs. They get the royalties from composing and publishing. And Joe gets his piece for being the leader. So what do I get for all my labour? A lie that I'll make almost two thousand dollars.

JOHN'S TOUR DIARY

May 18 (p.m.)

I'm writing this, my last entry of the tour, in the post office. Joe just informed me that my journal has been deemed a threat to the band. Well, fuck that! What the hell has happened to us anyway?

When we first started out we were united around a common goal. We hated the way the world had become. Capitalism, oppression, prejudice, censorship—these were things we rallied against. And the fact that popular music ignored these issues made us all the more resolute. We knew we couldn't change the world, but we at least felt we could be a part of something good.

I remember the first time I met Bucky Haight. He was sitting in Joe's kitchen, singing the smartest songs I'd ever heard. And he wasn't just going on about the negative. He was *so* positive. He had answers, solutions. I remember looking at Joe and feeling this huge sense of strength. And it was *that* strength which originally fueled this band.

When we were listening to Bucky the other day I remember looking over at Joe, wondering what was going on in his head. I remember his blank stare, that glazed look. This was a Joe I'd never seen before. It was as if he was lobotomized. There was nothing left. Nothing.

This reunion tour appealed to me because I felt the time off had done us some good—particularly between Joe and Bill. It seemed that we'd all mellowed a bit, that we'd all learned from our past mistakes, and that we could all get back to where we started. It makes me sick that I could have been so wrong. It's the same old shit all over again. A triumph of selfishness, ignorance, and stupidity. This is the worst mistake I've ever made in my life. And it breaks my heart to have to mail this home.

A MESSAGE FOR BILLY TALLENT

PHONE ED FESTUS.

COLLECT.

BILLY HANGS UP THE TELEPHONE

Right on, Ed Festus! You've finally come through! The lead gui-
tar gig in a grunge-metal super-band. Now I can get off this retro
shit hayride.

Of course Joe will be pissed off. I'll wait 'til the show's over
before I tell him. Man, I know he'll go rank. But, shit, who gives
a fuck? I've carried that guy for most of my life.

I mean, I've got to look after myself, right? And I know I don't
want to play this crap anymore. Joe will always be Hard Core
Logo. It's time to get out there and look after me.

BILLY TALLENT LIVE ON CJSR

INTERVIEWER: I'm sitting in the studio with Hard Core Logo's lead guitarist, Billy Tallent. Hard Core Logo are just completing the last leg of their all-acoustic reunion tour and will be appearing tonight at the O-Zone . . .

BILLY TALLENT: That's right, come early 'cause we're opening.

I: Billy, welcome to E-Town.

BT: The Canadian capital of rock 'n' roll worship. Glad to be here.

I: Well I suppose you guys have been getting this question a lot, but why did you decide to reunite?

BT: It was Joe's idea, really. We were asked to play a benefit in Vancouver and Joe felt the ol' magic was still there.

I: Whose idea was it to go acoustic?

BT: Joe's.

I: Billy, you were known as one of the loudest players in punk at one time. Three Marshall Hi-Watts on stage or something like that, right? How did you feel about going acoustic?

BT: Not so good.

I: Well, what convinced you?

BT: Nothing convinced me. I guess I felt I owed Joe one last tour on account of the fact that I broke his nose at a show in Toronto.

I: Billy, what do you mean by that?

BT: Well, this is probably the last time I'll play with the band.

I: How does the others feel about this?

BT: I don't know. I haven't told them yet.

I: Whoa! You heard it here first, listeners. Another CJSR rock talk exclusive.

BT: What's the big deal. I mean, we've made a career out of breaking up.

I: Yah, but we've never heard it from you before, Billy.

BT: True.

I: So what's gonna happen this time?

BT: Well, as for myself, I think I'm gonna get back into something with a heavier sound. I like speed metal and grunge a lot. I might do that.

I: I read an interview with your old manager, Ed Festus, in some L.A.-based skate mag last month, and he was saying that he was involved in a lot of that Seattle-sound stuff lately. In fact, it was the same interview where he mentioned you in his top five best thrash guitarists. I think you came in fourth.

BT: Cool.

I: What are your current influences right now? Any bands you like in particular?

BT: No bands, just sounds. I like the guitar sounds coming out of the Pacific Northwest; but I like the mass appreciation of those sounds even better. This could be the season for guitar feedback and distortion. I'd like to make it big with that.

I: Make it big?

BT: Yah, I wanna make it big. I wanna be famous. Don't you?

I: Yah, well . . . you're a punk rocker. You play in Hard Core Logo. You're not supposed to want that.

BT: After tonight I can want anything I want.

MAJOR LABEL REP

Hey, how're you guys doing?
Remember me?
I used to be in retail,
but now I'm a rep
for _____ Records.
Yah, so I wasn't busy tonight
and I thought I'd come out
and cheer you on.

I'm still hoping to get into A&R;
and when I do you guys will be
the first band I sign to the label.
You're not really my thing,
but I think you're way cool.
Here, take my card.
Have a great show.
Ooops! I mean break a leg.

BILLY'S ANNOUNCEMENT
JUST BEFORE SHOWTIME

After this gig
I'm catching a flight:
the 8:32 for Seattle.
I just made a deal
with Ed Festus Inc.
to form a new band for Sony.
I'm meeting the singer
on Monday.

EDMONTON BLOCK HEATER

Plug me in to your block heater
My mind's gonna take itself for a walk
It's goin' upstairs gonna take a breather
And it won't be home 'til after dark

Cold wind blowin' off the icy river
Up a-hundred-and-first to my back door
You'll keep me warm 'til six in the evening
And I'll see you tomorrow with my foot on the floor
At a quarter to eight not a second more
And I'll check on you at half past four

    She's been so good for me
    She's always there throughout the day
    Twelve volts a day

Take me out of this frozen season
Send me down south for a holiday
I'll spend some time in Costa Rica
'Cause I just can't wait to get away

And if I miss your block heater
Then I'll send for you by Fed Ex mail
And I'll plug you in 'til I think of leaving
Just the two of us sitting in the shade
Of a big palm tree on a sunny day
Ahh! It's twenty below are you okay?

JOE, THIRD SONG IN

This is a very special night tonight.
Not only is this the last night
of our hugely successful reunion tour,
but it's also the last night
of Billy Tallent's life.

SOMETHING'S GONNA DIE TONIGHT

I've got a bullet in my pocket like a Barney Fife
And I'm saving it up for the right occasion
Like tonight feels pretty good alright
So all's I've gotta do is get me a gun
And stare down the barrel and set my sights
Then squeeze the trigger 'til I feel that thud
'cause something's gonna die tonight

Well there ain't no use in trying to talk
It's been this way since the Rock of Ages
Rolled downhill and came to a stop
And bogged us down with it's extra baggage
That comes with the church and the man on top
And the daily grind for a better wage
That holds us up until we drop

　　Yah something's gonna die tonight
　　There'll be no peace, there'll be no fight
　　There ain't no point in wrong or right
　　When something's gonna die tonight

Ah, but what do you do when you get let down
By a person or a place or some thing you've trusted
Well you put up a fight 'til what's lost is found
And if you get beat up and your heart's all crushed in
You reach for your bullet and you wait around
For whatever it is that's got you busted
To get in sight, to hit the ground

THE 3:10 A.M. STORY

Look, guys,
before I say anything

I've got to say I'm sorry.

The owner's wife
came in at last call
and robbed the till.

Man, if I could give you all
one piece of advice
it would be

never do business
with a couple divorcing.

Ladies and Gentlemen,
Joe . . .

THE WAY PIPE FEELS

Paid in quarters.
This is ridiculous.
Hard Core Logo's
very last gig,
the promoter pays us
in quarters.
Makes me feel
like a busking band.

JOHN GOADS JOE

So Billy caught his plane
to Seattle, eh?
Just unplugged his guitar,
walked off stage,
into a cab,
gone.

Didn't even wait to get paid.

Must be nice
missing the drive
when the guy at the wheel's
got a knife on the dash.
Eh, Joe?

WHAT'S BREAKING UP AS COLLEGE RADIO NEARS THE CITY LIMITS

And for those of you who missed the acoustic Hard Core Logo reunion at the O-Zone last night, let me tell you all that you not only missed an excellent show but an excellent example of four people who have nothing better to do than whittle away at our student loans when we could be spending them on text books and laundry detergent. We all laughed when those legends of the sixties came back from the dead. Now we can laugh at ourselves as we cling to the nostalgia of . . .

Edson
Hinton
Jasper
Valemount

JOHN TO JOE

You know the problem
with you Joe
is that you're all wrong
from the start.
If the point of this tour
was to make ourselves
and everyone we dealt with
as miserable as possible,
then this tour would have
been a complete success.
The only thing different
from this tour and the others
is that the rest of us
have outgrown
the usual bullshit.
We're just going through
the motions, going
from moment to moment.
There's no vision left
to carry us
between the highs and lows.

At least Billy knows
what he wants.
I can't blame him
for leaving.
It's me 'n' Pipe
who look stupid,
trusting you to be, like,
the custodian of
whatever goals we set
when this band began.

PIPE TO JOHN

What about you, John?
You smug little fuck.
Where do you get off
harping about this band
falling apart?
Look at *you*.
You think 'cause you've got
one foot in and one foot out
that that's okay.
You're a fake, man.
I look at you on stage,
having a good time,
having one of your "moments."
Then I see you writing
in your little book,
analysing the down side
or whatever the fuck
it is that we're doing.
When I agreed to do this
I knew what I was
getting into.
I knew I'd get pissed off
at a lot of things,
but I also knew
what kind of money
we could make.
And I *need* the money.

This band means more
to the crowds it plays to
than it ever will to me.
And the fact that I get paid
to make people happy

is totally cool.
Who gives a fuck
about a vision?
Who gives a fuck
about Billy?
I'm just doing
what I'm doing
and getting paid for it.

Avola
Clearwater
Kamloops
Merritt

JOE TO HIMSELF TO BILLY

This is it, isn't it, Billy?
It's really over now, isn't it,
Billy?

Hope
Chilliwack
Surrey
Burnaby

May 25

Dear Joe Dick,

On behalf on the Green World Coalition, I'd like to thank you and your band for participating in our benefit show. Although we didn't make as much money as we anticipated, we at least raised the profile of our organization in the community.

I'm sorry about the misunderstanding that occurred between Pipefitter and Rainbow Trout, our M.C. You'll be happy to know that his front teeth have managed to re-root themselves and are no longer wobbly. If Pipefitter would be willing to send him a written apology, I'm sure he would consider dropping any legal action.

Please let me know when you guys are playing again. My twelve-year-old daughter just picked up a second-hand copy of *Son-Of-A-Bitch to the Core* and has expressed an interest in seeing the band live. Hope your tour went well.

Sincerely,

Laura Cromartie

June
July
August
September

LADIES AND GENTLEMEN, JOE . . .

My name is Joe Mulgrew.
I used to go by the name
of Joe Dick, singer
for Hard Core Logo.

I'm looking for three hot players
—bass, drums, lead guitar—
to form a kick-ass rock band
committed to recording and touring.

If you are under thirty,
seasoned and hungry,
then I want to hear
your very best stuff.

Send me a tape
of your hottest licks
and I'll tell you
if you've got the goods.

MICHAEL TURNER was born in North Vancouver, B.C. in 1962. A veteran of the Vancouver music scene, he helped form the hillbilly punk band Hard Rock Miners in 1987. *Hard Core Logo* has been adapted to radio, stage, and a film directed by Bruce McDonald. Michael is also the author of two poetry books, *Company Town* and *Kingsway*. He lives in Vancouver.